D0229702

Written by Gaby Goldsack
Illustrated by Steve Smallman

This edition published by Parragon in 2009

Parragon
Queen Street House
4 Queen Street
Bath BA1 1HE, UK

Copyright © Parragon Books Ltd 2003

All rights reserved. No part of this publication may be reproduced, stored
in a retrieval system or transmitted, in any form or by any means,
electronic, mechanical, photocopying, recording or otherwise, without the
prior permission of the copyright holder.

ISBN 978-1-4054-1502-6
Printed in China

Muddy Puddle

Illustrated by Steve Smallman

Bath New York Singapore Hong Kong Cologne Delhi Melbourne

It was a sunny day on the farm. The animals were hot and thirsty. Farmer Fred whistled cheerily as he carried his bucket to the water tap.

Farmer Fred turned on the tap. It whistled and clanked, but no water came out. He turned on every tap in the farmyard, but not a drop of water came out.

"I don't believe it," he called to his wife, Jenny. "There's no water!"

"I'll phone the Water Board," said Jenny.

Meanwhile, Patch the Sheepdog set off to check on the sheep. But as he passed Hog Hollow, he heard a grunting noise.

"My muddy puddle has dried up," Polly Pig complained. "If I don't get a mud bath soon I'm sure to get sunburnt."

"I'll fetch Farmer Fred," barked Patch. "He'll think of something."

"Trembling tomatoes!" cried Farmer Fred when he saw Polly Pig. "We need to make a mud bath. But there's no water in the taps."

Just then, he heard Dotty Duck quacking.

"I've an idea!" said Farmer Fred. He picked up his bucket and began to fill it with water from the duck pond.

"Quack, quack!" cried Dotty Duck crossly. There was hardly enough water left for the ducks to swim.

"Hmm, I'll get water from the brook instead," decided Farmer Fred.

Farmer Fred fetched two buckets of water from the brook and carried them back to Hog Hollow. He tipped them into Polly's dried up muddy patch, and then went to fetch some more.

Up and down, up and down he went. But when he stopped for a rest, he couldn't believe his eyes. Hog Hollow was as dry as ever!

"Bouncing buckets! It's drying up faster than I can fill it!" cried Farmer Fred.

"Well, perhaps Harry Horse can help," thought Farmer Fred. But when Farmer Fred fixed two buckets over Harry's back, he simply dug in his hoofs and refused to budge.

"Neigh! Neigh!" he complained. It was far too hot to work.

"Oh, dear," said Farmer Fred, fanning Polly with his hat. "How are we going to make you a mud bath?"

Never fear, I've an idea!

Just then, he spotted a length
of hosepipe curled up beside
the milking parlour.

"Never fear!" he cried, "I've an
idea!" And, grabbing the hosepipe,
he raced back to his workshop.

Farmer Fred bashed and crashed around inside his workshop.

Before long, the door to the workshop swung open. The animals stood back as Farmer Fred pushed out a strange machine with the hose attached.

"This," explained Farmer Fred,
"is a pump-action, sun-powered Puddle
Filler. We'll soon have the biggest mud
bath you have ever seen."

The animals followed Farmer Fred at a safe distance as he pushed the Puddle Filler down to the brook.

"Whatever is he up to now," neighed Harry Horse, shaking his head.

Everyone held their breath as Farmer Fred flipped a switch on the Puddle Filler. It spluttered into life.

"Now, just wait for the water," cried Farmer Fred. But nothing happened. No water appeared. Not one drop.

"Ah! The hose must be blocked," said Farmer Fred, peering down its end.

Suddenly, the hose began to hiss and squirm.

"Popping parsnips!" cried Farmer Fred, as the Puddle Filler reared up and chased him around Hog Hollow. Everyone scattered as it snaked and flapped this way and that.

Farmer Fred landed with a bump next to Polly Pig.

"It doesn't look like you'll be getting your mud bath after all!" he said. Then, Farmer Fred felt a drip fall on his head.

"Hurray, it's raining!" he cried, and burst into song...

"Woof, woof," barked Patch, looking up at the tree above the pigsty. Farmer Fred looked up. It wasn't raining. The hose was stuck in the tree and a cool shower was falling over Hog Hollow.

Just then, Jenny appeared at Hog Hollow with some good news.

"The Water Board said there was a burst pipe. It's fixed now, so the taps should be working."

At that moment, water gushed out of all the taps in the farmyard. Before long, Polly, Patch and the other animals were jumping in all the muddy puddles.

"It never rains but it pours," laughed Farmer Fred.